Text copyright ©2021 by Sheetal Sheth
Illustrations copyright ©2021 by Lucia Soto

For more information, please contact:
Mango & Marigold Press
hello@mangoandmarigoldpress.com

Library of Congress Control Number: 2021908842
CPSIA Code: PRT0621A
ISBN-13: 978-1-7370550-1-3

Printed in the United States

Bravo Anjali!

WRITTEN BY
SHEETAL SHETH

ILLUSTRATED BY
LUCIA SOTO

Take your space and *dazzle*, littles.
For E&M, the glitter of my life and N,
who's always the first to shine the light on us.
—S.S.

To my sisters.
—L.S.

"I'll bet Anjali knows. Right, Anjali? Why don't you show us since *you're* the star student." Deepak taunted.

All eyes were on Anjali.

Anjali was confused. She wasn't trying to show off. She was just playing tabla, like everyone else. And why was Deepak being so mean lately? She thought they were friends.

Anjali danced her fingers across the tabla to perform the composition in question.

She closed her eyes and got lost in the music as she always did.

UGH!

Anjali heard someone groan and she stopped playing.

"I guess I don't know it that well after all."
Anjali said sheepishly to the teacher, Zakir uncle.

Her stomach was doing flip-flops. That wasn't true. Not even a little.

Zakir uncle's eyes narrowed. He looked like he was about to say something, but changed his mind.

"The recital is next week everyone. Keep practicing, especially your solos. I will be announcing the winner of the contest. Someone will get to perform on stage with me at my next concert!"

Anjali packed up quickly.
She wanted to catch Deepak
before he left.

As Anjali hurried over to Deepak,
she overheard him planning a
practice session with the others.

When she finally made eye contact
with him, he purposely looked away
and walked off.

At home, Anjali was setting up her tabla to practice when she heard, "Beti, you are such a sweet girl setting that up for your Dad!"

Anjali looked up to see Heena auntie, one of Mom's friends, smiling at her.

This wasn't the first time someone assumed she didn't play the tabla. She didn't care that people thought it was a boys' instrument.

Anjali knew there was no such thing.

"Actually Heena, it's Anjali's," Dad boasted. "She's the chief maestro in this house — in charge of all the music *and* magic!"

The next day at school, Anjali overheard Deepak whispering to Mary. "People are only interested because she's the only girl in tabla class and they want her to feel special. She's not that good—."

Deepak stopped talking when he saw Anjali looking at them.

"Deepak, why are you—" Anjali didn't get to finish.

"Listen up class!" Mr. Malcolm clapped his hands. "We need a group leader for our next project. Who'd like to be in charge?"

Deepak saw Anjali raise her hand and abruptly called out, "I'll do it!"

"Hey- he can't just pick himself. That's not fair!" Courtney argued.

"That's not fair!" Deepak mimicked Courtney.

"STOP! IT!" Anjali said sharply to Deepak.

"Hey, everyone settle down!" Mr. Malcolm called out.
"Is anyone else interested?"

The class was silent.

"Alright then, why don't you both be in charge? You can be co-leaders."

Anjali excused herself and went to the bathroom.

Anjali took some deep breaths but she couldn't relax.
Her heart was pounding.

Tina, one of the 5th graders, came out of the stall and saw Anjali.
"Are you ok?" she asked.

"I'm just having a bad day." Anjali stammered.

"Why? What happened?"

"MY FRIEND SINCE FOREVER
isn't MY FRIEND ANYMORE
AND SOMEONE SCRIBBLED SHOWOFF
ON MY FAVORITE NOTEBOOK
IT'S NOT MY FAULT THAT PEOPLE MAKE A BIG DEAL
ABOUT ME PLAYING TABLA
I MAKE MISTAKES TOO
BUT I WORK REALLY HARD
MAYBE HE SHOULD TOO
HE SHOULD BE LESS MEAN
AND PRACTICE MORE
IF I WIN THIS CONTEST
NO ONE WILL TALK TO ME AGAIN
HE WILL TURN EVERYONE AGAINST ME
I DON'T WANT TO SEE A TABLA
OR HEAR A TABLA
OR PLAY A TABLA
EVER AGAIN!!"

It was quiet a moment.

"Never dim your light, girl."

Tina handed Anjali a tissue and walked out.

It was the day of the recital
and the hall was buzzing.

Anjali was in the bathroom
trying to calm her nerves.
She had decided that she may
not win the contest, but she
was going to do her very best.

She thought about the first time she ever saw someone playing tabla. His hands and the beautiful sounds he was creating had mesmerized her so much, she had come home and made her own tabla set out of old yogurt containers!

She wasn't going to let *anyone* make her feel bad for being good at something. Especially something she loved as much as tabla.

She had dreamed of a moment like this.

She reviewed the compositions in her mind
and looked at herself in the mirror.

"I can do this."

Everyone performed as a group first.
Then came the solos.

When it came time for Anjali's solo,
she closed her eyes and blocked
everything out.

Anjali was brilliant.

When she opened her eyes, she saw the audience standing
and cheering: "BRAVO! BRAVO ANJALI!!"

Zakir uncle congratulated her on stage.
She had won!

Deepak walked up to Anjali. "Congratulations."

"Thanks. Your solo was great, Deepak." Anjali said sincerely.

"Yours was better." Deepak admitted.

They both were silent.

"I'm sorry for how
I've been acting..."
Deepak finally said.

"You really hurt my
feelings, Deepak."
Anjali said honestly.

"I shouldn't have acted
like that. I was jealous.
I wanted to be the best,"
Deepak said bravely.

"I really am sorry, Anjali.
Hey, maybe you can
give me some pointers?
My fingers get so tired!"

"Sure, but mine do too!"

They both laughed.

As Anjali took one last look at the stage, she felt a tap on her shoulder.

"Bravo Anjali!! Bravo Anjali!!"

She turned to find a little girl looking up at her.

"I didn't know girls could play tabla," she said.

Psst! You know there's another Anjali book right?!

always **Anjali**

Sheetal Sheth
Illustrated by Jessica Blank

Sheetal Sheth is an acclaimed actress, producer, author, and activist.

Despite being told she'd have to change her name to work, her successful career has trail-blazed paths for other women of color across media. Sheth supports marginalized communities not only through her own pioneering work as an actor, but by also appearing at workshops and panels and speaking directly to issues facing those communities. She is known as an outspoken advocate and has had op-eds published on *CNN* and *The Daily Beast*. She served in AmeriCorps and is currently on the advisory board of Equality Now and an ambassador for The Representation Project. *www.sheetalsheth.com*

Lucia Soto is an illustrator living in London and working all around the world.

She was born in a seaside town in northern Spain and she grew up in a Mediterranean port city. She has explored and lived in different places and these days she can be found in her drawing room, surrounded by tropical plants and drinking tea from chipped teacups.

Lucia is fascinated by people and their journeys through time, she loves mystery and adventure and she spends her days drawing things that are half nonsense and half all sense, the stuff that makes her life silly and beautiful. *www.luciasoto.com*